JUDY MOODY AND FRIENDS
Searching for Stinkodon

Megan McDonald
illustrated by Erwin Madrid
based on the characters
created by Peter H. Reynolds

CANDLEWICK PRESS

In memory of my dad

M. M.

For Melanie and Mariel

E. M.

Text copyright © 2019 by Megan McDonald
Illustrations copyright © 2019 by Peter H. Reynolds
Judy Moody font copyright © 2003 by Peter H. Reynolds

Judy Moody®. Judy Moody is a registered trademark of Candlewick Press, Inc.
Stink®. Stink is a registered trademark of Candlewick Press, Inc.

First edition 2019

Library of Congress Catalog Card Number pending
ISBN 978-0-7636-9997-0 (hardcover)
ISBN 978-0-7636-9998-7 (paperback)

19 20 21 22 23 24 CCP 10 9 8 7 6 5 4 3 2 1

Printed in Shenzhen, Guangdong, China

This book was typeset in ITC Stone Informal.
The illustrations were created digitally.

Candlewick Press
99 Dover Street
Somerville, Massachusetts 02144

visit us at www.candlewick.com

CONTENTS

CHAPTER 1
The Big Dig

Dirt was flying. Dirt was sailing. Dirt was exploding in every direction.

Stink stopped digging. He looked at all the holes he had dug in the backyard. Swiss cheese city!

His sister, Judy, ran out into the backyard. "Whoa," she said. "You have dirt all over your face and in your ears and on your mouth. Are you digging your way to the other side of the world or something?"

"Or something," Stink said with a big grin. "I'm digging for a *Smilodon* tooth."

"Smile-o-who?"

"*Smilodon.* The saber-toothed tiger. Actually, they're not tigers. They are saber-toothed cats—prehistoric mammals that prowled the earth millions of years ago."

"Whoa," said Judy.

"They had these giant curved teeth, twelve inches long!" Stink clacked his teeth together, imitating the saber-toothed cat. "Mega-chomp!"

"Stink, I hate to tell you this, but the chances of you finding a saber-toothed anything are—"

"I know. I know. Like one in a gazillion million. But two kids in Michigan fishing for crayfish in a backyard stream found a mastodon bone.

"And a girl in Great Britain found a pterosaur bone and got it named after her. It could happen."

"Yeah, and I could get an A-plus on my spelling test," said Judy. "Or ride the London Eye Ferris wheel with the Queen of England."

"Hardee-har-har," said Stink. "Still, I could make the find of the century. Just think: I'll be on the cover of *Science Kid* magazine, and you will be Nile-green with envy."

"Snagglepuss," said Judy, slumping her shoulders.

The next day, Stink went back
to dig, dig, digging. His best friend
Webster came over and helped Stink
search.

They dug all day. They dug through what felt like seven hundred mosquito bites and seven thousand dandelion roots. At the end of day two of the Big Dig, all Stink had found was a bottle cap, a pile of acorn hats, and a 1985 penny. Webster found Judy's Where's Waldo? glasses.

On day three of the Big Dig, Judy came downstairs to breakfast. She poured a bowl of cereal. "Pass the milk, Stink."

"Can't," said Stink.

"Okay. *Please* pass the milk," said Judy.

"Gone," said Stink. He held up the empty bottle. He pointed to three empty glasses. Stink had downed one, two, three glasses of milk in a row.

"Piggly-wiggly," said Judy. "What's with all the milk, Stink?"

"Milk makes you strong," said Stink. He flexed the muscle in his arm. He squeezed the muscle in his arm. "I need to be strong for digging."

"Stink? Are you really going to dig up the backyard all summer? Come on. Let's go swimming for a change. Or start a dog-walking business. We could make piles of money." That would get Stink for sure.

"No can do. I have to keep searching."

"Don't you have karate today?"

"Karate will have to wait. Today's
the day. I feel it in my bones."

He started out the back door. "This
time, I'm not coming back inside
until I find something."

Judy rolled her eyes.

"Saber-toothed cat, here I come."

CHAPTER 2
Sneaky-Peaky

The Moodys' doorbell rang. Judy answered the door. It was Stink's other best friend, Sophie of the Elves. Sophie was dressed in her karate uniform.

"Hey, Judy," said Sophie. "Is Stink ready for karate?"

Judy shook her head. "Come look," said Judy. She pulled Sophie over to the kitchen window. They looked out

into the backyard. Stink was still out there, dig, dig, digging away.

"It's like a prairie dog town out there," said Judy.

"Planet of the Anthills," said Sophie.

"I've seen Stink hunt for Bigfoot and moon rocks and pirate treasure and asteroids," said Judy. "But he's never been as cuckoo over anything like he is over this saber-toothed tiger tooth."

"Wow. You're right," said Sophie. "Stink never misses karate."

"He thinks he's Indiana Jones," said Judy.

"Or Virginia Stink," said Sophie, giggling. "Maybe he'll find a crystal skull."

"He says he's not stopping until he finds something. But by then the whole backyard could cave in. The house will get swallowed up in one big gulp and we'll fall into the center of the earth and come out through a volcano or something."

"Hmm," said Sophie, scratching her head. "This is serious."

"Yes," said Judy, scratching her own head. "Hmm . . ."

Judy looked at Sophie. Sophie looked at Judy. "We better make sure he finds something," they said at the exact same time.

"Are you thinking what I'm thinking?" Judy asked.

"I don't think so," said Sophie. "But I can tell you have one of your crazy-good ideas."

"I'm thinking . . . *we* put something in the backyard for Stink to find.

He gets his dinosaur tooth or bone or
whatever, you get your friend back,
my family gets our yard back, and
I get a partner for my dog-walking
business."

"It's win-win-win-win!" said Sophie.

Judy and Sophie snuck into Stink's room.

"You be the lookout," said Judy. "Make sure Stink doesn't come up the stairs."

Judy looked on his desk and in his toy box and under his race-car bed.

"What exactly are we looking for?" asked Sophie.

"Something to bury. It has to be something that looks like a saber-toothed tiger tooth. Something that looks way old. Dinosaur old."

"How about a bone?" asked Sophie.

"All I have is my collection of wishbones," said Judy.

"Too flimsy," said Sophie. "How about a bone from that game where you operate on Cavity Sam?"

"Too plastic," said Judy.

"How about a bone like the kind a dog chews?" asked Sophie.

"We don't have a dog," said Judy.

"Shh!" said Sophie. "I think I hear something!"

"Footsteps!" said Judy. "Hide!" They ducked behind the wheel of Stink's bed.

They listened. Judy's heart pounded. Silence. "False alarm," said Judy.

"Phew," said Sophie. She peered at a picture of Stink on his dresser. In it, Stink had his head stuck through a life-size cutout of Daniel Boone. Stink was wearing a fake, fuzzy fur hat and a bear claw hung from a cord around his neck. "Hey!" said Sophie. "How about the bear claw Stink's wearing in this picture?"

"Great idea!" said Judy. "Except he lost it a while back when we were

trying to break a world record for the longest Human Centipede."

"Bummer," said Sophie.

"You just gave me an idea!" Judy inched open the top drawer of Stink's desk.

"Eureka!" said Judy, holding up a pointy gray tooth. "A shark tooth!"

"But it's so small," said Sophie.
"Saber-toothed tiger teeth are this
long." She grabbed a ruler and held it
out in front of her.

"Okay, so we'll say it's a *baby* saber-toothed tiger tooth."

"Great idea!" said Sophie.

"Now all we have to do is drop it right near where Stink is digging," said Judy.

"And make sure he finds it," said Sophie.

"For sure and absolute positive," said Judy.

Judy and Sophie went out into the backyard. Stink was kneeling in the dirt, still digging.

"Stink, look who's here!" Judy said.

"Great!" said Stink, waving Sophie over. "Grab a digger." He pointed to a pile with a shovel and a hoe and a rake and a plastic sand-castle shovel.

Sophie grabbed a small orange
digger with a blue handle. She
picked a hole, knelt down beside
it, and started digging to make it
deeper.

Judy slunk over to Sophie and
slipped her the shark tooth. When
they were sure Stink wasn't looking,
Sophie dropped the tooth into the dirt
where she was digging.

"Hey, Stink," Judy called. "Why don't you try digging over here by Sophie? I have a good feeling about this spot. I can feel it in my bones."

"Nah," said Stink. "I've already been over that section. All I found were rocks and more rocks and a squirmy worm with no head."

Stink went back to digging. Judy and Sophie put their heads together and whispered.

"He's never going to find it," said Judy.

"What do we do?" asked Sophie.

"If Stink won't come to the shark tooth, we'll have to take the shark tooth to him."

Judy plucked the shark tooth out of the dirt.

"Be careful," whispered Sophie. "We don't want him to suspect us."

Judy strolled over to where Stink was digging. She knelt down at the edge of his hole and peered in. She pretended to search the dirt for the saber-toothed tiger tooth. As soon as Stink looked away, she dropped the shark tooth into the hole.

Sneaky-peaky!

Judy drifted back to Sophie of the Elves, trying not to look guilty. "I did it!" she whispered.

"Perfect!" said Sophie. "Now, we wait."

CHAPTER 3
Saber-Toothed Surprise

Sophie went back to digging. Judy started digging in another spot. They dug. They waited. They did not have to wait long.

"Eureka!" Stink cried for all the world to hear. He pawed at the dirt with both hands.

"Wow! Is it by any chance a shark tooth?" called Sophie.

Judy nudged her.

"I mean a *baby* shark tooth," said Sophie. Judy elbowed her again.

"I—I mean—" Sophie stammered.

"This is no baby tooth," said Stink. "This is big. Really big."

Stink started to scrape the dirt off. "It's something hard, that's for sure." Stink scraped off some more dirt.

"Huh?" said Judy.

"Huh?" said Sophie.

They ran over to Stink.

The chunk in Stink's hand did not look like something Judy had just put in the dirt a few minutes ago. It looked like something that had been in the

ground for a hundred million years!

How did the shark tooth get so covered in dirt? Judy wondered. Sophie wondered the same thing.

"Maybe it's a bone," said Stink. "Or a fossil. No, wait! It feels curved, like a tooth. I think it's shaped like a saber!"

"Whoa!" said Judy.

"Whoa!" said Sophie.

"Whoa," said Stink. "I think I found something. For real. I think it's the tip of a tooth from a million-year-old saber-toothed cat."

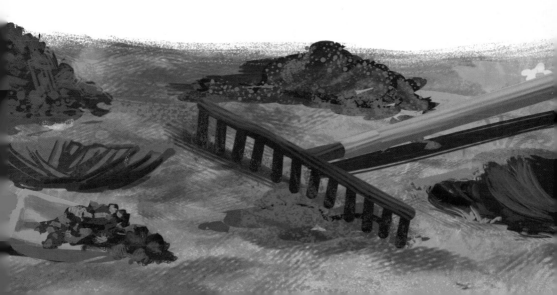

Stink scraped off more dirt. In his hand, Stink held a three-inch-long, curved, grayish-brown thingy that *did* look like a tooth, but not the one Judy and Sophie had planted.

Judy and Sophie looked at it, their eyes wide. Sophie was remembering the Daniel Boone picture of Stink. Judy was remembering a Human Centipede, when everybody was tripping over one another and falling down and Stink lost his bear claw in the Moody backyard.

"Whatever it is—it's definitely *not* a bear claw," said Judy.

"Definitely not," said Sophie. "It doesn't look anything like a bear claw."

"Just think," said Stink. "This could be, like, a million years old." Stink turned it over and over in his hands, imagining. His mind stretched back millions of years, all the way to the time of great woolly mammoths and saber-toothed tigers.

Stink hunched his shoulders and crouched like he was a tiger. "I am *Smilodon,* the saber-toothed cat, twice as heavy as a lion. I lurk in the forest primeval. I hide. I wait. Along comes a hairy mastodon and I, *Smilodon,* let out a loud roar. Grr! Rowl!"

"ROAR!" Judy added.

"Quicker than a blink," Stink went on, "*sproing!* I strike and attack my prey, stabbing it with my deadly teeth. CHOMP! I, *Smilodon,* break a tooth."

"Whoa," said
Sophie, picturing
Smilodon in
Stink's place.
"Do you
think if I put
this under my
pillow, the Tooth
Fairy would come?" Stink asked.
"The *Triassic* Tooth Fairy maybe,"
said Sophie.

"You mean Cenozoic," said Stink. "Right?"

"Sure, if you say so," said Sophie, shrugging. "Maybe the Cenozoic Tooth Fairy will bring you million-year-old money."